WHO SHOT

THE SHERIFF?

III

DEAD MEN TELL NO TALES

An Original Story

By

INTERNATIONAL BESTSELLING AUTHOR

JOHN A. ANDREWS

CREATOR OF

RUDE BUAY

RENEGADE COPS

AGENT O'GARRO

DESIREE O'GARRO

&

A SNITCH ON TIME

10/25/19

Published in the U.S.A. by
Books That Will Enhance Your Life

A L I
Andrews Leadership International
www.ALI Pictures.com
www.JohnAAndrews.com

ISBN: **9781793274199**
Cover Design: ALI
Front Cover Design: ALI
Optioned by ALI Pictures in January 2019

THE WHODUNIT CHRONICLES

WHO SHOT *THE* SHERIFF?

III

DEAD MEN TELL NO TALES...

TABLE OF CONTENTS

CHAPTER 1

Debris from thunderous explosion skyrockets and floats toward the night sky. Followed up by a residual of dense smoke and acidic fumes. Fire flames heighten from multiple cell blocks, aligned as a horseshoe. Meanwhile, in the distance, sounds of sirens and vehicular horns crescendos. Westview Penitentiary yellow and red fire engines race toward the South Wing. There, mostly female inmates lodge. Their estrogenic pow-wows intensify. It sounds like Anguish 101. The East and West blocks scorch.

Firefighters barge out and unlock cell doors aided by crowbars. Mega water laden fire hoses assume their aerial position, hoisted from the engine. They forcibly dowse the compound. Few inmates make it out alive.

In the intervening time, at the Eastern cell-block, marked units one thru fifteen. Agile firemen evacuate multiple inmates.

Unfortunately, Cell's sixteen thru twenty, nestled on the cul-de-sac hosts the roasted remains of its dwellers. The rancid scent like barbecue meat permeates. Among the roasted dead is Deja Nichols aka Yuki, originally from cell number sixteen. Her body gets pulled from the rubble. Deja was arrested on narc charges and co-chairing a Glock reconstruction entity. Her vicious death occurred just one week before boisterous, notorious Marcus Davis was set to be tried for shooting and injuring her. That failed to kill accident occurred months ago during a narc deposit which Davis orchestrated from behind bars. It was widely circulated, Davis had people on the outside doing his dirty work.

As a result of those prison fires, the next morning her third degree burnt corpse, along with five other inmate's travel in body-bags to the prison morgue on a flatbed truck and aided by some rough looking prison personnel.

Ironically, Deja's husband, Gregg Nichols, was recently released from cell # 11 in the East Wing, at least a city block from those fires. That's where the male prisoners were housed. A block known for housing newbies, life sentenced recipients, along with some hardcore veterans like Nigel, locked away for life on multiple rape convictions.

It wasn't long ago, Gregg Nichols, accused of the shooting death of Milton Rogers, bid farewell to those holdings after his acquittal. How could someone kill his close friend and mentor? Some questioned. Plus, the colleague to Rogers' friend, Grammy winner Wesley Haynes? How could he? The double-questions lingered.

For Rogers' death, 12 jurors found Gregg Nichols not guilty. Instead, Quentin Daley, the courtroom officer was sent to prison for that rubout. Many inside that courtroom, saw Milton Rogers mysteriously gunned down while testifying on behalf singer Wesley Haynes. Yes, Gregg Nichols did serve time, until he was able to beat the wrap. As a result, he was now a free man. Destined to put his life back together again. However, it seemed like bad karma was in pursuit of Gregg.

Yes. That story would have had a happy ending but salt was abruptly added to that wound as Gregg prepped for his wife's funeral.

Gregg Nichols was cut down in cold blood by a gunman outside The Rose Garden flower shop on Front Street in downtown Miami. His carnage for hours decorated the sidewalk with a wreath in each hand. That perpetrator is still at large.

One eyewitness claimed: the gunman disappeared in a no-license-tag bearing, Land Rover. A vehicle, similar to the make and model frequently used by the Jamaican Police Department or JPD.

CHAPTER 2

As these incidents saturated the Newscasts in the Caribbean the US. Late Fresh Breaking News interrupted with this coincidental complex story:

"Hair particles cited as experiments in the Wesley Haynes trial reportedly matched the head-hairs of Claude Weeks..."

The deal with the Sheriff and his Deputy should have been buried. However, the boogie man mentality was paramount in the mindset of Jamaican law enforcement. As a result, Quentin Daley was imprisoned and like vultures, law enforcement wanted more blood out of this episodic trial.

Claude Weeks was the pastor along with his wife, who according to police were first responders on the scene, immediately after the Sheriff and his Deputy was slain over a year ago.

In the meantime, while Claude was arrested, police raided his house. There, they came up empty. The raid soon extended to the church where he presided as pastor. Inside his office drawer, they retrieved a Glock 38. A handgun which was restored and housed similar bullets used in the shooting of Sheriff John Brown and his Deputy Ron Charles. Claude arrested without bail and awaiting to stand trial in the multiple murders, was found dead inside his cell. According to an autopsy result hours later, Claude reportedly died of a related heart ailment.

Additionally, Rose Best-Parsons' fingerprints were lifted from the Pina Colada fragrance canister found in the SUV pulled from the ravine, believed to be owned by the late Milton Rogers. Her DNA was found on a tube of red Lip Gloss, plus hair sample on the mat under the driver's seat. Meanwhile, Claude Weeks' hair sample was found on the passenger seat.

Rose, recently arrested outside a Mandeville Salon seemed appalled; regarding the charges brought against her. Convinced this case was already dead and buried, she was aghast when confronted with this ghost and placed into handcuffs.

"It wasn't me!"

She shouted.

Meanwhile, many clients at the salon which she owned and managed, felt she shot the Sheriff and his deputy to even the score with her husband's killers. It's still indelible in her mind while she was handcuffed.

Bill Parsons, her late husband was taken out execution-style while in Rose's company over a year ago at their music studio.

So, now in this elongated saga, two individuals were still tied to the case as complicit. In the meantime, according to an independent investigation the late ally of the Sheriff: Deputy Ron Charles' home was searched and the computer server which stored beats, as well as songs belonging to Bill Parsons Studio, were recovered. Was Deputy Ron Charles in on his boss' killing? Both officers were slain at the same location. That cover-up? Will we ever know? It was no mystery, multiple individuals were implicit in the Sheriff's assassination.

Were multiple individuals complicit in the murder of the Sheriff and his Deputy? If all alleged, those acquitted and those who were already dead were involved in those two brutal murders, law enforcement had their hands full with multiple pencil *erasers*.

Despite tainted investigations, *like the glove doesn't fit:* this whole thing should have been laid to rest. Instead, it resurged like a cat with nine lives.

With all these late but new findings permeating the news media and festering like stage four cancer masticating moment by moment. Law enforcement in Jamaica was caught with its hands tied or as some would say: like a dog with its tails between its legs. Did they drop the ball? It's obvious, they were forced to reopen the Who Shot The Sheriff? Along with his Deputy's case.

CHAPTER 3

This resurrected uncanny set of inexplicable entangled circumstances were poised to begin tugged back inside the courtroom in exactly six weeks from now. Jury selection now a work in progress.

On the other hand, The Jamaican Labor Party wanted to have the trial conducted in Jamaica. Juxtaposed to the opposition party The People's National Party which contested that move, preferring a Miami trial. They fought back and forth like the Democrats and Republicans during the 2018-2019 government shutdown. Fearing if the case was Jamaican tried, there would be grave repercussions. Like causing pandemonium and heated uprisings, street riots as well as shootouts. Consequences, they feared would affect their chances of toppling the Jamaican Labor Party during the upcoming general election.

In reverse, the Labor Party questioned the validity of re-routing this trial, now on its third go around back to Jamaica.

"If they are going to try Jamaicans, it's time to do it on the home turf."

Articulated by numerous legal experts.

To them, it was like a homecoming party, filled with media, courthouse spectacle and tourists.

"Anything for the bottom-line," voiced the Jamaican Minister of Tourism, bent on raking in the almighty dollar.

Through it all, most locals wanted to put the Who Shot The Sheriff? trial to bed and never shift the covers. Even so, Jamaican Law Enforcement wanted answers badly. They sensed there was a needle somewhere in that haystack and were determined to find it even if they got pricked deeply. Justice in their opinion had to be served, go high or low. Their elasticity was on steroids.

In the meantime, there were some locals who dreaded it all with a ten-foot pole. Distancing themselves in their minds provided solace. It wasn't putting food on their table nor paying their very expensive JEP light bills. So, they couldn't care any less.

Supporters of the Jamaica Labor Party felt if the first trial, which was supposed to be held in Jamaica – did. The Jamaican Mogul Milton Rogers would not have been shot.

They debated: *Quentin Daley, born and raised in Miami, and the Court Officer, perpetrated gunman accused of pulling the trigger which snuffed out the mogul Milton Rogers.*

Some also queried: *"If that case was tried on Jamaican soil like it was supposed to, there's no way a court officer would have pulled that trigger." His shooting tactics would have been easily detected before he found the right trajectory through that crowded courtroom.*

Others deliberated: *"He would have taken into consideration before pulling off such a feat that it would carry major consequences. As the Don would target his family and all his friends in order to implement community justice as well as the country's political agenda."*

Some cynics still believe it's a myth. However, most intellectuals beg to differ; in Jamaica, a Don run things. Inside out, next to the prime minister, He looms large. In the case of "Sponji Edwards" a Don who hails from Tel Aviv, Jamaica, and sub planted in Mandeville. Notorious and rambunctious in nature, and recently changed his name to "Glock Edwards." Sponji has become known now by many, as the Don who orchestrate the reconstruction of Glock 38s along with his co-conspirator Deja Nichols.

Additionally, Sponji controls the politicians, the guns, the shots, the bleach, and the money redistributed in communities such as Mandeville and Tel Aviv. In some cases, he is known to have access to more rounds of ammunition than the police and even a more eclectic collection of weaponry as well as cohorts.

Pre-trial proceedings rolled on with Rose Best-Parsons' name making headlines moment by moment.

CHAPTER 4

Wesley and Britney Haynes, currently on a European tour, were saddened when they learned Rose Best-Parson had been arrested and charged in connection with the murder of Sheriff John Brown and his Deputy Ron Charles. Knowingly, the circumstances they endured before their acquittal. They arguably showed their frustrations: 'It could never be Rose Best Parsons."

They debated without having all the facts to support their perceptiveness.

Even so, the Haynes' couple chose to detach themselves from the entire debacle as fingers remained pointed at them by some locals, especially in the Law Enforcement circles. Although they were acquitted of those crimes more than a year ago the scars of two trials involving the Sheriff still showed when it came down to Wesley Haynes' state of mind.

Nevertheless, according to News sources, Wesley stated:

"We still feel an existent bond with Rose Best-Parsons. It was Rose who opened the door for me in preparation for my musical career's first interview. I'll always be grateful to Rose Best-Parsons and her late husband Bill Parsons."

The News Media immediately launched into overdrive, covering multiple related stories. A female Miami judge Linda Lopez was picked, not based on Jamaican politics but by the US-based prosecution team.

The 12 Jurors made up of seven men and five women were now in place. The trial was inching closer. Rose Best – Parsons the only known defendant alive and about to be tried for the double homicide. If convicted she would face the death penalty. The discussion marinated and festered throughout the media.

On the other hand, multiple questions surrounded Sponji Glock's relationship with Yuki Nichols. Was he her mentor who flipped and orchestrated her untimely death? Also, it was widely speculated the two were having an affair while her husband Gregg Nichols was incarcerated. Gregg, no doubt died with those two wreaths in his hands as an exhibiting of his love for Deja. He held on to her in life despite her rumored triangular affair. In death, he was digging in, visibly with those two farewell treats.

Reportedly, Sponji Glock Edwards, affiliated himself with Yuki Nichols after Gregg Nichols, her husband, was imprisoned on charges for the shooting of Milton Rogers.

It was claimed: Sponji also supplied Yuki with narcotics, bankrolled her operation and endowed her with the rights to the reconstruction of Glock 38s. When it was leaked Yuki had inside information on who really shot the Sheriff and his Deputy, she was roasted in her cell at Westview Penn.

Police for years have been trying to bring down Sponji Edwards. He proved slippery as an eel surviving multiple assassination attempts by law enforcement.

However, they were never allowed to do their jobs properly because The *Don* dominated in several communities. Known as a community protector, he kept his own peace.

According to one insider:

"When it comes to the politicians, too many questions could be asked about drugs in Jamaica, with few answers to suffice. Those answers could be incriminating. So, many cooled their lips."

CHAPTER 5

While many questions were unanswered politically and legally, mostly those concerning the rise and fall of Bill and Rose Best-Parsons' empire stayed inside a vacuum. This not only troubled most whose bread basket was musical entertainment but some legal scholars as well.

They were known to have provided a huge musical payday. As alleged: Why were Rose Best-Parsons' fingerprints and lip gloss found inside the vehicle believed to have been implicated in the rub out of Sheriff Brown and his Deputy? Was Rose Best-Parson having a steamy affair with Milton Rogers after her husband's death? Why was her lip gloss found inside the SUV owned by Rogers? Reportedly, Rose could have used that vehicle to commit the murders. Was Milton Rogers the driver and Rose Best-Parsons the trigger pulling heroine?

According to sources, Rose came from a family of massive wealth. Her parents were plantation owners in Portland, St. Mary, as well as the hills of Manchester. She was their only child and the heir to their kingdom. Therefore, she inherited a large slice of their pie.

The Aston Martin which Bill drove and was shot up ferociously when Bill was gunned down. One source claimed: Rose gave those *wheels* to Bill for their 25th- anniversary gift. For years this gift caused a sore eye to many underachievers.

Additionally, sources claimed, the recording studio was also purchased by her, not Bill, as he seemed to make Wesley Haynes assume. It appears Bill Parsons ran things but Rose Best-Parsons was the real Boss Woman. She held the keys to the empire. After her arrest, law authorities drilled down deep to find out if Rose and Bill really did invest heavily in the narcotics trade which originated in Mandeville as some were insinuating. Still, no paper trail indicated such investments were made by this entrepreneur couple. Plus, the real estate which her parents owned in

Manchester was sold off prior to their death. Rose delighted in cash and she inherited much of it.

Even so, Bill, told Wesley Haynes, he diversifies and does not believe putting his eggs in one basket. The fact remains: Was he fabricating to Wesley, or all along, putting up a front to indicate what Rose had was his also, as both of them were one, blanketed like two peas in a pod.

During her arrest, Big Bubba who had worked with the moguls as engineer and chauffeur for many years was present when Rose was arrested. He recently pulled up a late model red Lamborghini. A car he drove to shuffle the boss woman. Bubba had tanned somewhat, grew a beard and wore his hair in a ponytailed style. A complete makeover from the look displayed on the day Bill Parsons was gunned down. Bubba at the time was also questioned by police but there was nothing he could be tied to in relation to the Sheriff and his deputy's murder.

CHAPTER 6

Inevitably, the media could not get their hands out of the *what-ifs* till. The deeper they drilled down the richer this mysterious Alfred Hitchcock type real-life mystery loomed. There were more probabilities to this case than anyone could shake a stick at. Not forgetting the number of dead witnesses as well as their co-conspirators.

During this new installment of the saga, Court Officer Daley, who is now locked away for life in the shooting death of Milton Rogers inside that Miami courtroom on Valentine's Day stated:

"I had nothing to do with the deaths of Sheriff John Brown and his Deputy Ron Charles. I am as innocent as a newborn baby. Other perpetrators are still being tried. So, there is no reason to keep me behind bars."

Not much attention was paid to his plea. As far as they were concerned, Quentin Daley was not charged and convicted in the assassination of Sheriff John Brown and his Deputy Ron Charles but he was, for the mogul Milton Rogers.

Meanwhile, new information surfaced: claiming Quentin Daley, while on vacation in Jamaica prior to the *rub out* of both officers, met privately with Glock Edwards at the Sandals resort in Montego Bay before returning to the US. Airline tickets and other travel receipts showed he met with Edwards at some of this Don's hideouts.

Text messages retrieved from his iPhone exposed it was Edwards who provided limousine transportation for Quentin to and from Michael Manley International Airport.

It was believed Daley could have picked up a Glock 38 from the Jamaican Don during his stay. The gun which some ballistics experts believe could have been reconstructed and the gun used to snuff out Sheriff John Brown, his Deputy Ron Charles, Milton Rogers and possibly Bill Parsons? All four key figures dead without any corroboration in this extensive real-life epic.

Multiple Legal Experts claim, "If Quentin Daley had ties to any of these four murders, Glock Edwards most likely supplied the Amu...as well as the intelligence."

As we recount these tragedies, mysterious findings surrounding the death of all four victims. The following Op-Ed which appeared in a Jamaican newspaper cited: "An individual filled with mystique, intrigue, and a reconstructed Glock could have been responsible for four deaths," authored by yet another prominent legal expert.

"If this is the case, and Daley is the gunman responsible, then there would be no need to hold Claude Weeks in prison,"

said a Church Elder caught up in the semantics of the Op-Ed. The Elder attended the same Wednesday nights prayer meeting at the church where Claude Weeks was the resident pastor. Conversely, with Quentin Daley demanding a release, many felt he did put his foot inside of his mouth. They sensed Daley knew too much about the narrative and seemed to be involved at a much deeper level.

On the other hand, Rose Best-Parsons should also be released if that Daley *theory receptacle* holds any legal water.

Still, some people probed: the police and prosecutor made too many blunders; people were imprisoned and the real assassin based on continued hearings was still out there. The name: Rose Best-Parsons emerged like sweet plasma and like a leech they were prepared to sucking her dry. Her holdings, if she was found guilty would no doubt be transferred to the Jamaican government.

Nothing changed when it came to the judicial process surrounding this case except, the government kept drilling down. They were moving ahead full steam, despite the existent suppositions. They were dug in on the *what if's*?

Law enforcement in Jamaica was gearing up for the gossip. While not receiving their marching orders for a local trial.

As many locals prolonged their demonstrations, hoping the winds of fate would change the judicial process and bring the savoring scent of the trial, directly under their noses, trial proceedings in Miami were salivating anyway.

CHAPTER 7

B ack home in Jamaica, demonstrators march around one of the most ancient landmarks in Mandeville, the Old Courthouse. A memorial erected back in the 1820s. The black, gold and green flag draped around the two pillars flutter and ropes the upstairs veranda. It accentuates both the Jamaican team spirit and patriotism. The protest quickly upsurges. If noise could help bring that trial home, they would be happy.

Who Shot the Sheriff? flyers, decorate the wall adjacent to the chain linked fence. The conundrum spikes, keeping out the riffraff.

Some signs feature ex-Mandeville native and platinum recording artist Wesley Haynes. The platinum recording artist, previously acquitted of shooting the Sheriff and his Deputy. Another depicts Glock Edwards the Don of Mandeville. Others pose a twin-pack featuring Rose Best-Parsons and Pastor Claude Weeks, the two remaining alleged cop killers.

In the meantime, a large group of Protestants, mainly students from the local church where Weeks served as a Youth Counselor assembled in a one-mile march heading toward the courthouse.

Meanwhile, on the courthouse grounds, an exterior air condition unit buzzed full blast. A large white sign hanging head-high reads: Ministry of Justice Mandeville Magistrate Court Office hours 10:00 A.M to 3:00 PM.

Closer, to the building a yellow sign with blue lettering reads: Urinating is Strictly Prohibited. Weed whackers and a clean-up crew speedily enhance the grounds.

An elderly man, part of Pastor Claude Weeks' congregation saunters on a walker. Looking on in anticipation he prayerfully expresses his desire for a home trial. To him, his deceased pastor should have some post-life intervention and procure a miracle to supernaturally bring the trial to the homeland.

Meanwhile, tourists inside idle taxicabs grab a few photos using their smartphones. Drive-by taxis honk their horns in a protest against the legal system. Locals in a huddle mumble in patois regard displayed photos of the alleged charged victims who were already dead.

CHAPTER 8

One week later, a huge crowd from just about every walk of life assembles outside. Boomed microphones pry over the heads of some placard bearing demonstrators. Media vehicles and journalists are poised to go LIVE.

Not long after the arrests of Claude Weeks and Rose Best-Parsons, the renowned journalist Bob Casey out of New York flew to Jamaica to see what juice he can squeeze out of the story.

Bob Casey, an American Journalist dressed in casuals, a Canon Sports camera strapped around his neck, and clipboard in his hand. He waits - poised.

A vendor chops away at a huge coconut using a cutlass. The client pays and partakes. While, police dressed in white shirts, and black pants with red stripe to the side and bearing M16 rifles, ambulate.

Uniformed court workers file in and enter upstairs of the courthouse. In the meantime: a remixed version of I Shot the Sheriff blasts from a spectating Millennia's iPhone. The teen continually puts the gadget to his ears and then removes it, matching the sound of the beat. All this goes into preparation for a possible Jamaican held trial. Moments later, it became breaking news as that pending Jamaica trial was shifted to the sunshine state and the city of Miami. When the news broke, it served as a tremendous disappointment to Jamaican locals. They protested some more.

IN MIAMI, outside the courthouse, a car pulls up. Attorney Stephanie Reid, representing Rose Best-Parsons steps out. Another car pulls up from which two escorts accompanying Rose Best-Parsons steps out. Instantly, boom microphones drop to accommodate. "Attorney Reid, how do you feel about your chances in this case?" asks one TV reporter.

"I feel great about our chances. Rose Best-Parsons is innocent as far as we are concerned." Says Reid with multiple folders underneath her arm. "Mrs. Parsons, you claim you're not guilty. Who do you think did it?" asks the Reporter. "I guess, that's what this case is all about. Finding out who did it." Says Mrs. Parsons. "Do you think they'll be finally able to put this case to rest?" At this point, Attorney Reid ushers her client to pass the courthouse entrance. An eclectic entourage follows in tow as she enters the courthouse stairs. The jurors are escorted inside by multiple guards.

CHAPTER 9

Back in Jamaica, after multiple weeks of stalling on the part of Glock Edwards, the Mandeville Don finally took the bait for an exclusive interview with New York's Journalist Bob Casey.

Bob enters the downstairs apartment after undergoing a search as well as close scrutiny by Sponji Glock's entourage. Customarily, a clipboard in one hand and his Canon camera around his neck. Oblivious to Glock's security team, the unit carried by Casey was already in record mode and flash disabled.

Glock, adorned with dark sunglasses and most of his face obscured, welcomes the New York Journalist inside a remote Kingston hideaway.

"How do you feel about all the tensions in Mandeville over the third go around in the same case?" Asks Casey.

"It is what it is Bob, life goes on."

Responds Glock Edwards.

"How long since you've been an activist for this Mandeville community? Your people seem to adore you?"

Casey asks.

"It's been 15 years since I man moved here from Tel Aviv in order to run things up in here."

States Glock Edwards.

"Have you ever seen it like this?"

Casey asks.

"No man! Like Bob said: 'Man to man is so unjust. You don't know who to trust. Some will eat and drink with you. Then behind them so-so pan you.' States Glock Edwards.

"Do you believe in the late Bob Marley?"

Asks Casey.

"Of course, the man saw things happening, happen and those things about to happen. And he knew the effects of them all."

Says Edwards.

"Things like what's happening in this, right *yah*, right now in this Who shot the Sheriff case? They should close this whole ordeal."

Says Glock Edwards.

'Is that so?"

Asks Bob Casey.

"Yes! The man even sang about such things to come. The only difference, Bob couldn't even shoot a fly. I guess he was referring to the anonymous. They say it was Wesley Haynes, Milton Rogers, Deja Nichols, Gregg Nichols, Claude Weeks, Quentin Daley, Rose Best-Parsons and a whole heap of us. They even said it's Eric Clapton because he sang *I Shot the Sheriff*. Even if he didn't write it."

Says Edwards.

"Do you know who might have shot the Sheriff and his Deputy?"

Asks Bob Casey.

"Things happen, people cool their lips, nobody is going to come forward...fess up? Dead Men? Dead Men tell no tales as far as I am concerned."

Says Edwards.

"Why not? Why wouldn't anyone fess up to these two murders?"

Asks Casey.

"What happens in Mandeville, stays in Mandeville. Just like what happens in Vegas stays in Vegas. You understand?"

States Glock, looking away as he attends to his ringing cell phone.

"Dread, me kinda busy right now. Let me call you back later. I have company. You no see?"

Glock says into the phone and hangs up. Casey interjects:

"So, you are not going to say who did it even if you knew?"

"I think Gregg Nichols was involved. He had access to the reconstructed guns. They were inside his attic. Why would anyone arm people with a pistol if you know you are going to use it to kill? Go figure. It wasn't Yuki. Ah, him whey arm Rosie with it."

Says Edwards.

"Thanks for talking with you on this matter regarding who shot the Sheriff? And his Deputy."

Bob Casey wraps up the interview.

CHAPTER 10

T he trial was now into its closing arguments phase. Bob Casey, apparently had no intentions of leaking the Glock Edwards interview to the media. He probably intended for it to air after the judgment in the case or on MSNBC High-liners. Thus, causing a wrench to be thrust into the end result, and creating chaos in the media.

Unfortunately, on his way back to MO Bay airport his car was rear-ended and shoved off the road collapsing in a deep ravine.

Several locals heard the crashing tumbling sound. Some saw the vehicle descend. Many responded to the rescue. Although they failed in an attempt to save Bob's life, they walked off with his camera equipment along with the interview footage. The automobile was later sawed open to extract Bob Casey's body.

Later that same night, the Glock Edwards interview footage ran on a local Jamaican TV station. Hours later, a Miami Cable Station followed suit. Law Enforcement in Miami swarm over the Late Breaking news like flies over molasses. Yet, no one claimed responsibility for leaking the news.

Many wished the news was released before the closing arguments, to have an impact on the trial. Most came to grips that the stable was already closed.

Even so, the defense went to war with the prosecution although the new evidence was inadmissible. Although, many claimed it had merit and could have changed the trial's outcome.

CHAPTER 11

Meanwhile, outside of the Miami Courthouse: multiple protesters demonstrate. they hip-hop. they swagger. they wave hand-made signs which read: *ROSE BEST-PARSONS IS INNOCENT, ROSE COULDN'T SHOOT A FLY, SET HER FREE-END THIS TRAGEDY.* They chant. "Free Rosie! Free Rosie!" A Vendor presses into the crowd handing out white T-Shirts. They read: FREE ROSIE. SHE'S NOT GUILTY.

News Reporters converge attempting to engage demonstrators. Protesters remain preoccupied.

An agile News Reporter lands and latches onto a DEMONSTRATOR, who's holding up a sign, reading: ROSE COULDN'T SHOOT A FLY.

"Hello. Are you anticipating a non-guilty verdict?"

Asks the Reporter.

"That's right. She didn't do it."

Replies the passionate Demonstrator.

Law Enforcement, including Court Officials, remain on high alert just in case the protest goes out of hand.

"What gives you that assurance?"

Asks the Demonstrator.

"Rosie wouldn't hurt nobody. We were classmates. She does not believe in violence. Plus, she's a total giver. She gave me a loan when I was struggling with buying my first car... Without Rosie, I'll still be on the bus."

Says the demonstrator as the protest crescendos.

Inside the Courtroom: Some court attendees file out perplexed. The Defense team, seated on the front row with closed folders wait in wonderment. The Prosecution sits parallel on other side huddling. They feel the odds are very much in their favor.

The defendant Rose Best-Parsons looks shattered still perched on the witness stand.

Inside the hot Jury Box, twelve seemingly tired Jurors reside. Some fan aggressively using their note-pads. Some look confused and sweating.

JUROR 7, a Jamaican man in his 50s looks vindictively savvy and antsy. While he chicken-scratches additional notes on a disheveled note pad.

JUROR 2, a short Napoleonic Latino in his late 30s seems overanxious as he constantly drones the courtroom clock while eying the clock on the wall.

JUROR 8, a woman of Jamaican descent powders her nose, primps her hair and applies bright red lip gloss.

JUROR 12, an Asian woman in her 30s seems distracted with matters of her own.

JUROR 6, a flaming French man steals notes from JUROR 5's notepad. He's an Australian man-40s.

JUROR 4, a man of Indian descent in his 30s seems unsure of himself and the court proceedings.

JUROR 3, a very opinionated Italian man in his 40s, peruses through his body of notes.

JUROR 9, an African American woman in her 30s pow-wows with JUROR 10, a Hispanic woman of her age. Meanwhile, JUROR 11, a Caucasian woman in her 40s is focused on the Judge.

The HEAD JUROR, a man of Caucasian descent scans through multiple note pads and then mops his brow with a large multi-colored hanky.

JUDGE LINDA LOPEZ, a Latino Woman in her 40s, finds herself doodling with her pen on a pad. She scans the court-room. Locked in on the Jury Box, she gavels. There's complete silence for a moment, and then Judge Lopez speaks authoritatively.

"Ladies and Gentlemen of the Jury... "

The Head Juror gives his undivided attention. Judge Lopez continues:

"You've seen the evidence and you've heard the testimony in this extensive and complex trial."

Rose Best-Parsons is poised; not sure of her fate.

"You've heard the closing arguments articulately presented by both the defense and the prosecution. A case in which two outstanding Law enforcement giants in Jamaica The Sheriff and his Deputy were gunned down in cold blood. If there's probable cause you should present a unanimous guilty verdict without any reservation."

She pauses as the Prosecution team chatters, getting their attention. They finally zeroed in on her reverently.

"If there's no probable cause you should deliver a unanimous not guilty verdict similarly. Now, I expect you to perform your duty and provide justice in this case. Premeditation murder is a serious charge and this trial certainly bears its DNA. It warrants the death penalty in our system. The jury will now retire and begin to deliberate with ambition, justice and integrity."

The Judge gavels again. The twelve Jurors Exit concerned.

CHAPTER 12

Additional Court attendees file out. The number of Demonstrators increase. They press close to the revolving door as some court attendees clear away.

They are louder than ever. Bearing extra signs: I SHOT THE SHERIFF, I AM THE GUNMAN, WHO IS THE REAL GLOCKMAN? Once again, News Reporters engage with demonstrators pressing for excerpts.

Signs billboard: DON MAN AIN'T NO KING KONG. LOCK UP THE DON MAN, HE'S THE GLOCKMAN. SET ROSIE FREE! NO JUDGE, NO JURY!

Back inside and above the held open door by a neatly dressed female GUARD. It reads **JURY ROOM**. The Jurors enter. The Guard displays her southern hospitality with colossal style and pizzazz.

A large conference room with a huge conference table and twelve chairs wait. The walls seem like they have recently freshly painted. Some Jurors irritated, blow their noses in disgust. One wall features a dry erase whiteboard with markers and an eraser in accompaniment. Another wall is mostly bare except for a detailed map of Miami on one side. On the next wall, a circular clock displays Roman numerals points at 5:00.

There are multiple windows. Some half opened from the top, except for the one with the NO SMOKING sign, kissing its ledge. The windows backdrop downtown Miami in an afternoon setting.

A kitchen sink houses a coffee maker for decoration sake. While a water fountain with paper cups inside a cup holder memorializes.

Two adjacent doors read Restroom/Banos. One reads Men and the other Women.

The Jurors are all in, and buzzing in pre-deliberation mode. Some are still sweating. The Head Juror surveys.

"Can you cool it down for us, a bit?"

He says to the Guard.

"Will do!"

The Guard responds enthusiastically.

The Head Juror, courtly:

"Thanks. We'll call you if we need anything."

The Guard surveys. She gets a head count and closes the door.

The male Jurors remove their jackets. Most Jurors take their seats. Some wander aimlessly while others huddle in pow-wow mode.

Juror # 5, hastily heads to the Men's room. Multiple eyes are focused on the huddle. In which, Juror 2 is preoccupied. He's grouped with Juror 7 at that no smoking sign window. Outside? Pouring down rain dominates.

Juror 7 turns to Juror 2 as he mops his brow.

"At least it's not so hot in here. It was hot as hell inside that juror's box. I couldn't wait to get out of there."

Immediately, Juror 6, lands in the huddle. He's flaming.

"I've never been to hell. The closest I came was watching that movie To Hell and Back but the theatre was air-conditioned."

Juror 7 eyes Juror 6 after that remark.

"Thanks to Jah Jah. His rain is here to cool us down. Come on and cool me down! Cool me down! "

Juror 2, weaves into window for a closer look at the pouring rain. Juror 6, follow suits.

Back at the conference table, other jurors pounce. Some add to their already collected notes.

The raindrops decrescendo. The element draws another onlooker - Juror 3, eavesdrops.

"The Heat plays tonight in all of this?"

Asks Juror 2 somewhat tellingly.

"Why, do you have tickets?"

Asks Juror 3.

"I wish we can hurry up and get out of here."

Says Juror 2.

Juror 7 says to Juror 2:

"These things, you never know how long they go. This one can be a marathon."

Juror 6 responds.

"Why? She's guilty as hell. Unless Milton Rogers stole her lip-gloss and planted it inside that abandoned SUV."

The Head Juror attempts bringing Jurors to order with a wave of his hand. That doesn't work.

"Excuse me, let's get down to business."

The cluster dissolves.

CHAPTER 13

T he twelve Jurors are back in their seats at the table. The Head Juror presides:

"As you know in this trial, we have a defendant who faces the death penalty. Guilty or not guilty, our verdict has to be unanimous. I believe we can get this over quickly and return the verdict to Judge Lopez."

Juror 12, seems disengaged and unmoved by the proceedings thus far.

"What's the rush? Aren't you going to give us time to recollect our thoughts and think about this case through?"

She asks.

"What's there to think about? She's as guilty like thunder follows lightning."

Says Juror 2.

Suddenly, Thunder blasts followed by lightning bolts.

"See? Even the elements are in sync. That's what I'm talking about. Team spirit!"

Continues Juror 2.

JUROR 9, shares her notes with JUROR 10. While JUROR 11, eavesdrops on their collaboration.

"Well, I guess we are ready."

Says Juror 9.

"I guess we are. Let's talk it through."

Agrees Juror 11.

The Head Juror zeros in on all twelve jurors, command order and then continues.

"If we are ready to let's do it or if we need to discuss it, so be it. Okay? Two, Three, Four, Five, Six, Seven, Eight, Nine, Ten, Ten? Who is missing?"

"What's his name? He went to Banos. I hope he finds it."

Says Juror 6. He draws unanimous attention.

"So, he got lost?"

Asks Juror 10.

"Poor guy. He must be suffering from TB. I mean Tiny Bladder."

Juror 2 insinuates.

Meanwhile, Juror 5 returns. He completes the drying of his hands with a white rag and takes his seat at the table, looking somewhat edgy.

The Head Juror is taken aback.

"Next time let us know. Will Ya? Not that we need to know. But we do. Do you know what I mean? We need to know where everyone is all the time. Including their votes."

He continues.

"So why are we here? That woman sure pleaded her heart out, for all I know…"

Juror 12 eyes him intently.

"So, you've already made up your mind?"

"I did not say that. I was just reflecting. Tossing things out loud in my mind."

The Head Juror retorts.

Juror 12 remains intent.

"You must be a writer. It is said: Writers think 95% of the time and uses the other 5% of their time to ink their ideas."

"How did you know? I am."

Responds the Head Juror. Most of the Jurors wish he left self-promoting out of the deliberation process. He feels their penetrative stare.

"So, as I was saying. The Sheriff and his Deputy are at a speed trap preceding the semi-lit intersection. Weather condition? Almost dark…"

"Dusk. We call that dusk!"

Interrupts Juror 8.

The Juror is persistent.

"Dusk or almost dark? Same thing according to a thesaurus. A dark SUV whisks on by. They follow ardently, sirens, flashing lights and all. The SUV tries to elude them. They wouldn't let up. Finally, the SUV pulls over. The sheriff's and his Deputy's car lights are still flashing. They park, get out and cautiously proceed towards the now idle SUV. Bang! Bang! Two shots rang out through the rear windscreen of the parked SUV. The Sheriff and Deputy are cut down. The SUV takes off through unlit Manchester streets."

Juror 4, raises his hands contentiously.

"Who witnessed those killings?"

He asks.

Juror 7 takes in Juror 4.

"No one."

To Head Juror, Juror 7 continues adamantly:

"It's all circumstantial evidence."

CHAPTER 14

The Head Juror continues on a roll.

"The Pastor and his wife showed up, pronto. Blood splattered along the roadside. Broken glass everywhere."

Juror 7 counteracts.

"We can't include the Pastor's statement. He's already dead. Deceased. Gone. Lifeless. They said it was a heart attack. Whatever the cause? Dead men cannot testify in a court of law. That's why he wasn't brought in..."

To that statement the Head Juror replies:

"I don't trust people who say they are Christians and don't live as Christ did."

Jurors 7 and 8 are caught whispering with each other.

The Head Juror is focused on Juror 7.

"So that's why you voted not guilty?"

To which Juror 7 replies:

"I am just exercising my right as a member of the twelve."

Juror 11 interjects:

"I can't believe we are still caught up in this red wave blue wave conundrum? Are you sure both of you think she's not guilty?"

Juror 7 and 8, nods yes.

Juror 11 shows her disgust with the Head Juror.

"If this continues, we could be here all night."

Juror 2 chimes in.

"I concur! All night long. All night long. I hope we end up Easy or Dancing from the ceiling."

"Ok. Let's try this again. This time we'll do it by ballots. I'll pass out a slip of paper to each of you. Please write your vote down, return it to me and we'll go from there."

Says the Head Juror.

"Before you do Mr. Head Juror. You are the Leader of us all. It's you who is designated to speak for all of us when we return to that hot jury box. I feel like we are wasting our time. Majoring in the minors."

States Juror 5.

He pauses, scans the room and continues.

"If they claim they are not guilty, we need an explanation. Find out why they feel the way they do. Don't you think? Judge Lopez expects us to deliver unanimously."

Juror # 2 looks first at the clock and then out that sign bearing window. He attempts to light up a cigarette but changes his mind.

Juror 7 asks Juror 2.

"You need a Nicorette gum?"

Juror 7 accommodates. Juror 2 takes 2 sticks of gum.

Juror 7 surveys the room.

"Any other takers?"

Juror 2 attempts to grab another. Yet, he changes his mind.

CHAPTER 15

The raining intensifies. Lightning flashes. Thunder rolls. The Head Juror focuses on Juror # 8.

"Please explain why you voted not guilty. Will you?"

Juror # 8 stands erect. She takes in everyone.

"I didn't see her do it!"

Multiple Jurors chuckle.

Juror 6 staring her down.

"Oh. Come on, lady. None of us did. That's the reason we are here."

"I was asked to speak on the matter. Now, do you mind if I continue?"

Says Juror 8.

Head Juror focuses on her.

"Please continue."

"Do you know who Sponji Edwards is?"

Asks Juror 8.

Juror 5 is all over it.

"He's the Don. That Jamaican Mafia who gave that last-minute interview to Bob Casey from the Cable News Channel... and later Casey was found dead."

"Bob Casey? Another dead man. They seem to have popped up everywhere."

Laments Juror 9.

The Head Juror gestures for Juror 8 to continue.

She does.

"Do you know what a Jamaican Don does? And no. He's not a Mafioso as you just described. A Mafioso is small fries compared to that Jamaican sweet potato."

Juror 2 raises his hand high.

Juror 8 ignores. All eyes are now focused on her.

Juror 8 continues.

"They are capable of installing a Prime Minister during a general election. They own more bullets than the Jamaican Police Department, more guns, more ammo and have more children than Abraham... and the twelve tribes of Israel. They populate..."

Juror 5 interrupts.

"Were those the same guys who killed Malcolm X, Peter Tosh, Tupac, and Big E?"

Juror 9 standing competitively:

"What does all this have to do with this case? Malcolm X?"

"Cockroach don't attend cock fowl party. I'm very happy with my vote: Not guilty."

Juror 8 states and take her seat.

You can hear a pin drop in the room after that remark.

Eyes engage those of other jurors.in slow motion.

Head Juror turns to Juror 8.

"Are you saying, if you voted guilty. The Don will come after you and your family and burn your house down?"

"I guess you can read between the lines. Ah, how the songs go? There are more questions than answers. I shot the Sheriff but I didn't shoot no Deputy."

Juror 8 responds. She gets up from the table, goes to the window, and looks out. She again sucks them into her vacuum of thoughts.

CHAPTER 16

The rain subsides. The Miami Harbor is now in clear view.

Juror 8 is still at that window and on a flow.

I can see clearly now the Miami Harbor from here. Invaders, Immigrants, a whole boatload. There's no southern border here. No wall. No steel slats. They must have come through Cuba or Haiti.

Juror 2 tries to interrupt her. She ignores his tactics and persists.

"How did the defendant's DNA get on that tube of lip-gloss? How did her prints get inside that vehicle? Why was only one strand of the defendant's hair recovered from that SUV, found abandoned in the ravine? You, don't mess with the Don. He's more lethal than Putin, Kin Jun Um, MBS and King Kong."

The Head Juror scratches his head as he cools his lips. Juror 5 jumps in.

"She has a point. If this guy, Sponji Edwards, the Don was sitting at the table when the first reconstructed Glock rolled out. He has the preeminence. No wonder he out-arms the police. He, says jump and the villagers ask How High? He installs Prime Ministers. Oversees drug cartels, Plus, he bankrolled the entire Milton Rogers Empire, which included nightclubs, hotels, casinos… I would dread him."

To which Juror 9 responds.

Another dead man. Milton Rogers, the conspirator. Who else is dead inside this cagy complex whodunit? Juror 7 informs Juror 9.

"Bill Parsons, Milton Rogers, Deja Nichols, Sheriff John Brown, Deputy Ron Charles, Gregg Nichols, and Bob Casey. So far."

"Will you let her continue, please?"

The Head Juror asks. Juror 9 interrupts.

"Why wasn't Sponji Edwards called to testify?"

Juror 4 responds:

"Because we only learned about his last-minute interview with Bob Casey during closing arguments.

How convenient? Plus, the US cooled its heels regarding Edwards' extradition."

CHAPTER **17**

Juror 3 is all wound up. He addresses Juror 7.
"Milton Rogers? What a closure to nothing? A man shot during his own testimony? What a debacle?"
Head Juror's eyes are fixed on Juror 7.
"Let's focus on the defendant Rose Best-Parsons.
Why is the defendant not guilty?"
We sense Juror # 7's uneasiness
Juror 7 zeroes in on the Head Juror.
"Where were you born?"

"Hollywood."

Responds the Head Juror.

Juror 7asks:

"Hollywood? So, you were in the movies? Did you get a taste of the Good, the Bad and the Ugly? Tinsel Town?"

"No. Hollywood, Florida."

Replies the Head Juror.

Juror 2 eyes the clock.

"Look at the time. Where are we going with all of this, to the full length of the court? I hope we are going to dunk. No missing that basket."

Using his hands, he immolates an arching free-throw shot.

Juror 7 continues:

"Mr. Head Juror, where I'm from, I didn't grow up flushing. I went to the out-house."

Juror 6 asks:

"Out-House? You mean the S - Hole?"

Juror 7 responds,

"POTUS 45 referred to it as an S - Hole country. If for some reason when I visited, I accidentally fell in. Not only will I had been submerged or trying to swim out of eight feet deep of… No plunger can bring me back."

Juror 11 squirms.

"By then not even the flush from a water hydrant can save me. Not even snaking could. So, why should I go down that S - hole with you? Why are you trying to take me down that slimy rabbit hole? Come on, I said she's not guilty."

Juror 6 whisks.

"How insensitive are you? A Rabbit hole can never be that treacherous, deep and slimy. That rabbit will forever lose its furry coat. She's guilty like that S-Hole is."

"She smells!"

Shouts Juror 2.

"Now where are we on the voting?"

Asks the Head Juror.

Juror 9, the African American female juror and Miami native raises her hands.

"Mr. Head Juror. I've changed my mind. Not guilty."

Juror 3 is ticked off.

"Who's adding to the pile?"

Juror 7 counters.

"Watch your mouth. That was relevant to my childhood not to my stance in this trial. I have the right to decide. I vote not guilty."

The Head Juror remains focused on Juror 9.

Juror 3 is animated.

"So, now you've joined both of them. Siding with them. We should have known you would. I saw it in your eyes when you walked through that door. Even the guard looked at you funny. Birds of a feather..."

Juror 9 reemerges.

"I don't have feathers. Neither do I flock. I just flipped. That's my prerogative. What's wrong with flipping. It might soon become our constitutional duty to walk things back. Well, I misspoke earlier... Finally, realigning what I said."

Juror 2 is calculative.

"Now we are 9-3. Nine for guilty. Three for not guilty. This is what I gave up the Heat vs Knicks for? Whatever happened to unity? Togetherness? United we stand. Divided we hang ourselves."

Juror 12 chimes in.

"We keep missing the bucket, the cup, the hole, the basket, whatever? It's becoming more evident: We do not understand how much this trial costs. Neither the sacrifices being made to come to a verdict. We can recoup the money. Time is something we can never get back."

The Head Juror writes on the dry erase board: 9-3 and articulates:

"I think it's time for a stretch break. Let's reconvene in two minutes."

They recess.

CHAPTER **18**

The Jurors mingle in multiple groups.
Near the sign-posted-window. Juror 6 groups
with Juror 7.

Juror 6 asks Juror 7:

"Where in Jamaica are you from?"

"Mandeville, Manchester."

He answers.

"You are in the thick of it all, aren't you?"

Juror 6 asks.

"Yep."

"Are they still rioting over the changed venue for this trial?"

Asks Juror 6.

"No. That's water under the bridge now. They are more focused on the verdict."

Juror 6 presses:

"I overheard you are a lawyer in the making. The bench on your mind?"

"Yes. Indeed."

Replies Juror 7.

"So, you think your home girl is not guilty?"

Asks Juror 6.

"How could she be? The evidence against her is insufficient and uncorroborated. Relatively, it doesn't matter what I think. It has much to do with what all 12 of us decides, unanimously."

Juror 7 defends.

"I've been to Jamaica. It's a beautiful country. I had such a wonderful time…"

Says Juror 6.

Juror 5 emerges and interrupts.

"I've watched cricket at Sabina Park. Played a few holes of golf. Love the food as well as the culture. You are a banker, I heard."

Juror 6 continues:

"Yep. I hated banking with a passion."

"Really. Why?"

Asks Juror 5.

Juror 6 responds:

"I've grown tired of counting another person's money."

Juror 5 responds

"Been there. Done that, Mate."

Juror 7 interjects,

"So, what keeps you busy besides playing golf?"

Juror 5 replies,

"Investments, portfolios, stocks, bonds, mutual funds. The whole shebang."

"So, you graduated from counting another person's money to now counting your own? That's a major step-up."

States Juror 7.

"Adda Boy."

Says Juror 6.

Juror 5 responds,

"Yep. Total freedom..."

Juror 12 joins the huddle and interrupt.

"Yep. Money and freedom sure go together. Extreme Money Makeover. That's what I teach my clients. Some get it. Some don't. Just like this whole deliberation process."

Juror 7 responds,

"I like freedom. Believe in freedom. I would die for freedom."

"You sound like MLK. I am happy to join with you today in what will go down in history as the greatest demonstration for freedom in the history of our nation. Close quote. The great deliberation. We're getting ready to reconvene."

Says Juror 12.

The other jurors are reassembling at the table. Juror 7 and 12 presses 5.

Juror 7 continues,

"So, how do you get sucked into this jury business? Locked away in a room with a large conference table, 12 chairs, eleven individuals who you have very little in common with?"

Juror 5 states:

"Justice. Mate. Justice."

CHAPTER 19

Jurors 5, 6, 7 and 12 head to the table and take up their positions.

Most jurors at the table seem more relaxed. However, Juror 2 seems preoccupied with happenings outside the deliberation room. The Head Juror gets his attention and presides.

"We've said much so far but not much to do with this case. Maybe that's why our vote is 9-3. A sheriff and his deputy are dead. We are here to determine if the woman accused of the crime is guilty or not guilty. Her fate has been placed in our hands. We are required to vote unanimously. Are we on the same page? Let's take another vote before we proceed."

Juror 2 contends,

"Yeah. Let's vote so I can catch up on the score. They've got to be deep in the last quarter by now."

Juror 5 shoots back:

"Don't worry. They'll get blown out by the Knicks in the final 2 minutes. Swish! Swish! Swish! Three-three pointers in the last minute. Game over!"

Juror 2 retorts,

"Not in Miami. Maybe at Madison Square Garden. Our home crowd is so ruckus, you can hardly hear the whistle."

Head Juror interjects:

"Please write your verdict on the piece of paper in front of you. Fold it in two halves and pass it back this way."

They vote.

Head Juror tallies up the votes. He articulates.

"It's still 9 guilty and 3 not guilty."

Juror 6 is unraveled.

"Unreal! I don't like disharmonies. I don't handle them well. It seems like we are further and further away from the plain truth..."

Juror 2 follow suits.

"It looks like we are going to be here all night long. I can't stand the waiting game."

Juror 2 leaves the table abruptly and goes to the window. He continues:

"When it rains it pours? I thought at least I would be able to catch the last minutes of the game. Anybody has access to ESPN or NBA TV?"

"Knock it off. Let's pull it together."

Says the Head Juror.

Juror 6 states:

"Yes. What do we know about the defendant Rose Best-Parsons?"

He proceeds to count his fingers.

1. Rose was born to wealthy parents - slave plantation owners.
2. She grew up with a gold spoon in her mouth.
3. She married the famous music producer and mogul Bill Parsons at age 17...

Juror 5 interrupts.

"What does all this have to do with this trial?"

The Head Juror intercedes.

"Let him finish. I hope this is all leading up to unanimity."

Juror 7 interjects:

"Come on! Have some faith in the process. This woman's life is at stake. Pzzzz, puff and her life is fried out of her like a drop of water in a hot frying pan?"

Juror 6 is agitated.

"If I may continue that would be great."

Juror 2 focuses his attention on Juror 7 & 6.

"Are you the new Head Juror? Give em an "EL" they take a Line. Come on hurry up."

Juror 6 proceeds.

Number...? Where was I?

4. Whoever killed her husband Bill Parsons, is possibly still at large.

5. Her wealth has more than doubled since her husband's death.

6. The Glock 38 which was recovered in her SUV was reconstructed. Her fingerprints all over it. The gun is a replica of the one found at Wesley Haynes' house after the Sheriff and his Deputy was killed. She stated the gun wasn't hers. Yet, her secretary testified that she always carried it inside that black, tinted glass beast of a car - Lamborghini. How did her secretary know it was there all the time and the defendant didn't.

7. Her DNA was found on the tube of red lip gloss, recovered from Milton Rogers' abandoned SUV.

8. The defendant testified, Sheriff John Brown was an obnoxious cop, who insulted her after a traffic stop. After which he issued her a ticket for driving above the speed limit. 'I was not even speeding.' She testified. Really? Come on!

9. Additionally, she said it was her assumption, the Sheriff knew who assassinated her husband Bill Parsons. She stated it was her opinion, the Sheriff knew every rub-out-bandit in Mandeville.

10. She's guilty as the rain follows the rainbow.

Juror 9 yarns and then responds:

"You have given us much to unpack. I hear what you are saying. Yet, none of us can prove beyond a reasonable doubt. It would be on my conscience to put this woman to death by a guilty vote. With that said: my vote is still not guilty."

Those jurors supporting a guilty verdict, become unraveled. Those supporters of a none guilty verdict maintain poise.

Juror 2 eyeing the clock.

"This is unreal. When are we going to agree unanimously?"

Juror 5 asks:

"Why don't they run the trial again so some of us can get up to speed? When are we going to look at the real facts?"

"We are for crying out loud!"

States Juror 6.

CHAPTER 20

Juror 5 is relentless.

"If she went on 5th Avenue and 42nd street in New York. Video security cameras surveilling the entire intersection. She pulled out her reconstructed Glock and shot up multiple pedestrians. Put the gun back inside her Gucci purse. She gets back inside her Lamborghini.

Most of you would still say she's not guilty. Why? Because she's got money. Lot's of it. Remember OJ? He was so loaded… so the glove didn't fit."

Juror 9 responds:

"Yeah. That glove sure didn't fit. No matter how much they forced it on. I wonder why?"

Juror 3 presses.

"Even if she paid me off. That woman is still guilty. Her motives are strong enough to personalize a vendetta and shoot the Sheriff. Realizing the Deputy was alleged although not charged for illegally acquiring Bill Parson's beats..."

Juror 7 interrupts.

"I guess he was planning on becoming a rhythmless reggae artist."

Juror 3 continues.

"Maybe. Resultative, the defendant immediately cut him down, feeling he had something to do with her husband's assassination. In my eyes, Rose Best-Parsons is guilty, guilty, guilty!"

"So, based on our recent decision, we now stand at 4 claiming not guilty and 8 for guilty. It seems we are now further away from being in unison..."

Says the Head Juror.

Juror 2 responds.

"This thing should have been over by now. We seem to be going one step forward and two steps backward. We can't find the basket. It seems like the hoop has moved to Orlando or New Orleans."

Juror 5 is animated and on his feet.

"I agree. Rose Best-Parsons had multiple motives. She was present when her husband was gunned down. She testified she wasn't able to identify his killers. It has been well-circulated law enforcement was involved. At the time Sheriff John Brown headed up the department. She, no doubt held on to the thought of the Sheriff's involvement. So, she stalked him. Located his speed traps. Then when the time was right on that night in August, Rose Best-Parsons sped by his hideout. Knowing that would provoke a chase. The Sheriff and his deputy took off in pursuit."

Juror 8 converses with Juror 7.

CHAPTER 21

Juror 8 is reddened.

"When did she find time to do all of that and run multiple businesses?"

Juror 5 states:

"She never said...

So, she pulled over to the curb and waited. The Officers got out of their cars and carefully walked towards her SUV. She saw them coming. As they got closer, she perfected her aim. Bang! Bang! Rose Best-Parsons shot both of them. Colored her lips red and drove away from the scene through a Manchester unlit street."

"I concur! Now we all can re-vote and get out of here. We've been breathing each other's air for too long." Says Juror 4 who has been silent for most of the deliberation. Juror 2 gives him thumbs up.

Juror 9 is adamant.

"Not so fast. Why would a woman color her lips after committing a double homicide?"

Juror 12 exclaims.

"The lip gloss was red. The color of blood is always red. Instead of having their blood on her hands. She placed it on her lips. So she can brag about it. The price for the alleged killing of her husband. Additionally, vowing to not telling the truth if she got caught. How sweet a vendetta. I can see that on a billboard in downtown Miami. How Sweet A Vendetta! The Cop Killer!"

"There's nothing factual about what you've just said. Come on?"

Says Juror 10.

The Head Juror tries to maintain leadership.

"Okay. Let's not get carried away. Remember, we are in search of a verdict which mirrors the evidence and the testimonies in this case. Anything else shows bias."

Juror 8 is up out of her seat.

"There are some facts pertaining to this case which we seem to have overlooked. Wesley Haynes was incarcerated. He was later put on trial and acquitted of these same murders. He's still alive, living large while bragging about his innocence."

Juror 7 zings her.

"Bill Parsons, the defendant's husband according to evidence, was assassinated weeks before both of these officers were slaughtered. Some have stated the sheriff could have had a hand in his slaying, even if they have no proof."

Juror 7 supports.

"Milton Rogers, the high-flying music producer was gunned down inside the courtroom next door. He was an amigo and an ally of Bill Parsons. Also, the man who gave Wesley Haynes his break to stardom.

Claude Weeks, the pastor?"

Juror 10 is intent.

"Was he really a pastor, a cover-up or a murderer?"

"That's what the evidence claimed. Weeks and his wife Doris were the first people on the scene while the blood of both officers was still pumping. Ironically, Claude Weeks hair sample was found inside that abandoned SUV owned by Milton Rogers. After spending a few weeks in jail, Claude Weeks suffered a heart attack and he's now a dead man. Departed! Deceased! Gone! Below Ground!"

Juror 5 tries to get in on the debate. Juror 8 is resilient.

"Quentin Daley was incarcerated for shooting Milton Rogers inside that courtroom. He also visited Jamaica during the time both officers were gunned down…"

"Where is all this taking us?"

Asks Juror 5.

Juror 2 is fixated on that clock on the wall.

Head Juror addresses:

"Let her address the matter, will you? There's some life in what she's saying."

Juror 8 continues:

"Deja Nichols, aka Yuki Nichols, accused of aiding in the reconstruction of the Glock 38. The murder weapon of choice. Subsequently, she was roasted inside her cell. Gregg Nichols, the choir boy, and her husband died on the streets of Miami. He was gunned down outside a flower shop with a wreath in each hand."

Juror 12 is fluid.

"Eighty percent of those accused are already dead. Who's alive to tell the tales? Plus, this trial is costing the US a fortune. If this was held in Jamaica, it certainly would have bankrupted their government."

Juror 8 stands in confrontation. She eyes Juror 12 despicably.

Juror 8 continues.

"So, what are you trying to say?"

Juror 12 chimes in.

"There's no reason to be offended. What I'm trying to say is Jamaica has sold just about everything it owned: Air Jamaica, the Bauxite company, the Sugar factory. What else? They even sold Red Stripe to Heineken for how much...? Maybe pennies."

Juror 8 is furious.

"You better watch your mouth!"

Juror 8 takes her seat.

Head Juror restores calm.

"Okay, Juror 12. As you stated in regard to Gregg Nichols, he was gunned down outside the flower shop... Let's stay on that track."

"That's right."

Says Juror 12.

Juror 8 responds.

"The only person alive to defend herself is Rose Best-Parsons. The truth she did tell. According to her: She does not know how to operate a handgun. With that said: I'm standing by my vote - not guilty."

The room is in an uproar. Jurors pow-wow.

Juror 2 wipes his sweaty brow.

"Why didn't you say you were of that same opinion five minutes ago? Because one of our fellow jurors alluded to the selling of some of the greatest Jamaican enterprises? You are biting in like a Pitbull."

Juror 8 rebounds.

"Jamaica is not on trial. A Jamaican woman who's not guilty of a crime she's accused of is. That electric chair will stay idle. She will not sit thereon."

The jurors are all ears. More so, the head juror. The debate slips into high gear.

Juror 12 is furious.

"Despite your patriotism, sentimentalism, and optimism about your country. The evidence, in this case, shows: Rose Best-Parsons committed those heinous murders and should face the electric chair."

Jurors voting guilty express affirmative mannerisms.

The rain is still pouring down buckets. Thundering has taken its boisterousness to a new level.

Juror now 5 has the floor. He's vibrant and thunderous, competing with the element.

"This is inconceivable. Women hunt. They fish. They visit the shooting range. Most gravitate to trigger-happiness during a heated argument with a significant other. One of my classmates related a situation to me. According to him. He was involved in a heated argument with his x-wife. She jumped up on top of the bed. Stood there. Raised the tempo to another level. He persuaded her to calm down. She didn't. He later jumped up on the bed. She lashed out at him. He tried blocking the blow. She later called the cop and said he struck her. I don't mean to sound sexist. Some women don't have an issue striking out when submerged with a vendetta. It's a given: Any woman who really wants to shoot, she shoots - Bang! Bang! If it's a man, she feels she's the big winner."

The female gender shows disdain over his domestic violence remarks. Anyway, he continues.

"The mere fact her fingerprints were lifted from the weapon in her possession indicates:

1. She practiced using it.
2. She used it to defend herself or
3. She used it to shoot Sheriff John Brown and his Deputy Ron Charles…

Juror 6 inching to say something since Juror 5 touched on that delicate story. Interrupts.

"Me? I've never used a gun, loaded a gun, been to a shooting range or owned a gun. Don't know how those things work. The closest I've come to one of those weapons was during this trial."

CHAPTER 22

The Head Juror recalibrates.

"Okay. Well, now that the gun thing has become an issue. Let's revisit the testimony of the ballistics expert. Shall we?"

Juror 7 jumps up. Other eyes penetrate him. He composes himself.

"According to the testimony of that ballistics expert: After putting the guns of Sheriff John Brown and Deputy Ron Charles through the same ballistics test, as was done for that of the defendant. It was determined according to the expert; those fatal bullets were similar to the ones found inside the magazine of that gun in the possession of the defendant. The expert later claimed all of the guns were reconstructed."

Juror 5 exhibits his discontent.

"The expert did testify: After shooting a bullet from the defendant's gun into that tank filled with water and then inspecting it under a microscope. The bullets which killed the Sheriff and his Deputy were analogous."

Juror 7 is back in stride.

"How did all of these reconfigured apparatus wind up in the hands of a civilian and law enforcement alike? Was it possible those two officers didn't want any evidence to leak or surface? Any evidence which could link them to other crimes using their guns? Was all this an attempt to suppress evidence? Make it untraceable. Make both the gun and the bullets untraceable?"

Juror 8 supports.

"That ballistics expert's testimony was the identical scenario he delivered when Wesley Haynes was tried for the murder of both officers. I feel like this is heading to another mistrial."

Juror 5 is combative.

"The reconstruction of the Glock, according to the second witness for the defense is nothing but a hoax, a witch hunt, a charade."

Juror 12 follow suits.

"I totally disagree. Everything about the reconstructing a Glock 38 was posted there on Google for the whole world to surf. Suddenly, after that same ballistics' expert testified for the prosecution and against Wesley Haynes, for those two murders, the link was instantly removed. Who did it is still unknown? I'm sure it wasn't China. Was it Russia that removed it, Saudi Arabia, Iran or Venezuela?"

Juror 6 states:

"I guess we'll never know.

The prosecution really had a good case until they began talking about the rebuilding of the Glock. Too much complexity. If they took all of that mumbo jumbo out of the case, they would have a chance of convicting Rose Best-Parsons. Focus on her motives..."

Head Juror turns to Juror 6.

"So, what are you saying?"

Juror 6 responds:

"What I'm saying, based on that cluster of evidence? I have to change my vote to a not guilty..."

"You are kidding me! We had this whole thing locked up. I thought a verdict of guilty was close until that restoration business was introduced into these deliberations. We'll never get out of here tonight."

Says Juror 2.

Juror 5 responds.

"Don't worry about that basketball game. The Heat is going to lose in the final two minutes. They'll choke."

Juror 2 senses a Heat loss.

"Don't count us out. We're resilient. A little momentum down the stretch? You know we can shoot the three ball like none other. Not even Golden State Warriors can compete when we get going."

The Head Juror gets up from the table. He goes to the board. Erases the 8-4 vote status with 7-5. The Head Juror is steadfast. There's a conclusion in his eyes. Bringing it home becomes paramount.

He remarks.

"Let's get a head count on the votes. I wished we all could be yea or nay unanimously, instead of stretching this thing elastically."

CHAPTER 23

Juror 10 turns to the Head Juror in disgust.

"I hate the voting process. It's irregular. Remember, the infamous Hanging Chards and Dimples across town in Broward County? Gore vs Bush 2000. Resulting in a Bush 271 electoral votes to Gore's 266."

Juror 7 responds:

"Chards and Dimples? ... sounds like a musical group to me. Broward County? It's still the same. Rick Scott vs Bill Nelson 2018. You can't get a good vote out of that place anymore."

The Head Juror responds.

"Okay. Let's leave politics out of our deliberations and get on with the vote. The clock is ticking. Juror 2?"

Juror 2 turns to Head Juror.

"I still say guilty. Guilty as a Pimp in a double-breasted suit!"

The Head Juror is intent.

"Okay. # 2 guilty. Juror # 3?"

Juror 3 says,

"Guilty!"

"Okay. # 3 guilty. Juror #4?"

Juror 4 says,

Guilty!

"Okay, # 4. Guilty. # 5?"

Juror 5 says,

"Guilty. She's guilty!"

Head Juror zeroes in on Juror 6.

"Okay. Juror # 6, how do you vote?"

Juror 6 says,

"I say guilty. And would not change my mind."

Juror 5 asks:

"So, you voted with most of the women. I wonder why?"

Juror 6 responds,

"Yes. Me Too, rules. I was selected out of a jury pool just like you."

"Calm down."

Says Head Juror.

Juror 6 is irate.

"Tell your Australian mate to calm down. He should mind his own business. This is not counting another person's money."

CHAPTER 24

The Head Juror goes to the water fountain and fetches a drink of water.

"You all are not making this easy."

"Whoever said this was supposed to be easy? The Judge said it was a complex case. This thing is filled with way too many probabilities. I guess she knew we would never reach a unanimous verdict."

States Juror 6.

Head Juror responds:

"She must have a Crystal Ball or believes in the serendipitous."

Juror 2 says:

"The Judge should have done this herself."

"Blame the ancient Greeks. They called it *dikastai* You are lucky there's not 500 of us in this room.

Head Juror responds:

Really? Dik-as-tai? Juror # 7, what's your vote?

Juror 7 answers,

"Not guilty. She didn't do it. Couldn't do it. She wouldn't do such a thing."

"Juror # 8, where are you on this?"

Asks the Head Juror.

Juror 8 responds.

"Not guilty. She didn't do it."

"Juror # 9, what's your vote?"

Juror 9 says:

"My vote is still not guilty."

"Juror # 10?"

Juror 10 says:

"Right now, I'm deadlocked. Please get back to me later. Sorry."

"Come on! That's not how it's done. You signed up for this didn't you?"

Says the Head Juror.

Juror 10 responds:

"Tough decision…"

Twenty-Two Jurors eyes are focused on Juror 10.

"You don't want me to guess, do you?"

Juror 6 responds:

"At least someone else has the guts to stand up. Although it's a bad roll of the dice."

Juror 12 is focused.

"Will you PLEASE stop trying to contaminate the Jury. Thank you."

Head Juror points at Juror 11.

"Juror # 11?"

Juror 11 answers.

"She's not guilty. I'm holding onto all my cards."

Head Juror asks Juror 12 her decision.

Juror 12 responds.

"Head Juror. You know where I stand in all of this. The wealthy always think they can pay their way out of a crime. Not on my watch. She's guilty."

CHAPTER 25

Juror 7, energized with sarcasm, states:
"The Heat just lost the game. It was a blowout."
Juror 2 scans the room.
"There is no Television in here. How did you find out?"
Juror 7 responds:
"It suddenly got very cold inside this room."
Juror 2 asks,
"It wasn't a complete blowout, was it?"
Juror 7 responds:

"No. The cold air keeps blowing from the outside. When it rains here in Miami, it's worse than Downs River Falls."

"That's an overstatement. Okay. Let's regroup and get back to the business at hand."

Says the Head Juror as he writes on the board 6-5-1.

He zones in on Juror 10.

"Juror 10 we need your vote. Are you ready with your decision?"

Juror 10 responds:

"I guess I would say she's NOT guilty. She couldn't have done it sleepwalking."

Juror 2 responds:

"Now we are tied. What a cumbersome series of missed layups? Now we're split right down the middle."

The Head Juror erases the stats from the board and writes 6-6. The 6 Jurors who voted guilty vacate the table and huddle at the water fountain.

The jurors regroup. Juror # 2 looks more frustrated than ever. He's so agitated, he paces. He's eyeing the clock.

"We've been making a go at this for hours. We are no closer than when we began. It seems we have drifted further away from the basket. We missed the lay-up, the dunk, the stuff. Now we can't even drain a free throw much less shoot from the top of the key. It's clear. The ball goes in. It ball bounces out. We fail to score points. We'll be here all night trying to score. This has gone into overtime. It could be heading toward double OT…"

Juror 5 interrupts.

"Yeah. It seems like some of us take this for a Cricketing Test Match. They don't play those anymore. It's now all in one-day games. Now the momentum has shifted toward a not guilty verdict. It is said: Momentum is hard to get and easy to lose. That's a truism. It doesn't matter if we keep voting until the cows come home. I'm still convinced. The defendant is guilty. She did it."

Juror 7 gets up, goes to the water fountain and gets a cup of water. He stays next to the fountain, drinks all of it. Throws the empty cup in the trash.

Juror 5 continues during Juror 7's absence.

"She shot the Sheriff and the Deputy. All evidence points to her. Her motives were clear. The Jamaican system had been very callous to her by orchestrating her husband's death. So, to even the playing field, she shot and killed both officers in cold blood."

Juror 7 returns to his seat at the table.

Juror 2 responds to Juror 5 comments.

"I'm with you. I like that kind of talk. She's guilty as hell. Why was she carrying a Glock if she didn't know how to use it and have never even shot a fly? Knowingly, it was the weapon of choice because it was reconstructed. On the other hand, not being able to trace the seller or the buyer is no excuse for her defense. According to the witnesses' testimony, two individuals in Jamaica initially had full access to the reconstructed handgun: Sponji Edwards and Deja Nichols aka Yuki Nichols."

CHAPTER 26

Juror 4 has the floor. He seems resurrected.

"That Yuki Nichols was some character, wasn't she? She lived a double life. How cool. What a masquerade?"

Juror 2 interjects.

"She was. Yuki was introduced to the music industry by Bill Parsons. The defendant's husband. As the witness further testified: Yuki Nichols went gangster after the rub out of the Sheriff and his Deputy. It was disclosed that on the day before those brutal murders, Yuki and Rose were seen at a club owned by the late

Milton Rogers in a lengthy conversation. Could it be possible Yuki Nichols was telling Rose Best-Parsons how to use the Glock 38? We don't know. The Sheriff reportedly visited the same club and threatened to shut it down. All we know is one day later, circumstantially, both men were killed with a Glock."

The Head Juror goes into note-taking mode.

"If one day after the meeting between Putin and Trump in Helsinki, the US suffered a major tragedy. Of course, Trump would be blamed. We have no way of finding out what was discussed between the two women. Just like we have no way of finding out what was discussed between those two world leaders. In the case of the sheriff incident. Yuki Nichols is dead."

"So how did the Deputy get shot?"

Asks the Head Juror.

"Like it was said earlier. The deputy got in the way. He wound up at the wrong place at the wrong time."

States Juror 2.

Juror 10 is robust.

"When asked why all the evidence found inside that abandoned SUV was not handed over to the crime lab? Detective Paul Stevens, while producing a picture of that abandoned SUV stated: The crime lab had full access to the vehicle for months. They should have swept it clean."

Juror 7 asks:

"Why not?"

He gets everyone's attention.

"It was evident they wanted to nail Wesley Haynes for those crimes. It seems Detective Jones and Stevens had it in for Wesley Haynes. It was all a botch job. For months that abandoned SUV was not recovered. When its locale surfaced. It was discovered nestled in a cobweb. This recovery occurred almost at the end of the Wesley Haynes' trial. So, you see why I'm sticking to a not guilty decision."

Head Juror asks:

"Juror # 9, why are you holding onto the decision of a not guilty vote?"

Juror 9 replies,

"When asked if she ever met Sheriff John Brown? The defendant Rose Best-Parsons said: She first encountered Sheriff John Brown one Saturday night in Kingston. He rolled up at a restaurant which was co-owned by her and Milton Rogers. He arrested several of her patrons, claiming they were prostitutes, pimps and drug dealers."

Juror # 7 urges her on.

Juror 9 continues.

"She further testified: upon hearing the commotion outside on the patio. She stepped out to investigate. The Sheriff was getting inside his car while the van with the arrested drove away. The Sheriff yelled: I'll shut this joint down. He later did."

Jurors listen intently.

"When asked her opinion of the Sheriff? Rose Best-Parsons said he seemed to be very shady.

When asked why she thought so? She answered Brown couldn't even keep a straight face. He couldn't look her in the eye during his boastful remark. She also stated: Moments before he showed up at the restaurant, Milton Rogers phoned her, complaining Sheriff John Brown comported in a similar manner. Many had a vendetta against him. He wasn't to be trusted. He was as crooked as a tree root.

Now they want to put her in a chair and flip the switch. Execute her? Have you ever in your existence witnessed a man being executed? I witnessed at least six."

"Never have."

Says the Head Juror.

Juror 9 continues. While Juror 11 visits the water fountain.

"You need to. Everyone who said she's guilty needs to."

Juror 11 fills a cup of water.

"He begs. He spits. He kicks. His eyes roll. He pisses and shits in his pants before he goes to the other side. Could you imagine what a woman does? Picture it! Picture a woman with her farewell white dress on. Well, if you haven't. Why are you asking me to change my vote?"

Juror 11 dumps the whole cup of water.

"That's grotesque. I'm changing my vote."

Says Juror 11 as she returns to her seat.

"Oh. Come on! Another one just bit the dust!

Says Juror 3.

The jurors become bedraggled.

The Head Juror writes on the board 5-7. He then commands order. Several Jurors remain disgruntled. Mainly Juror 2.

"We've made it out of 200 potential jurors. We are required to submit a unanimous verdict. Even if this thing goes for a week, a month, however long it lasts. It's our obligation."

Says the Head Juror.

CHAPTER 27

Juror 2 paces the room.

"I didn't sign up for all this. Who manufactured those rules? What if the jury gets choked? I mean hung."

Head Juror responds:

"That's not the result we are looking for. It says we aren't totally together in our voting."

Juror 3 is enraged.

"How many other police officers did Rose Best-Parsons rub out with that reconstructed Glock? We don't know. According to the evidence presented, the prints lifted from that gun matched the gun of Rose Best-Parsons - the defendant."

Juror 10 states:

"Do our hearts seek the truth or our minds? A good person produces good things from the treasury of a good heart, and an evil person produces evil things from the treasury of an evil heart. What you say flows from what is in your heart. Luke 6:45 NLT. The defendant said vehemently, 'I believe that the Pastor committed those twin murders. He claimed his wife and him were first responders. Claiming they were fresh from attending a prayer meeting at their church. What hypocrisy? No coincidence he died of a heart attack."

"Another dead man. The dead does not substantiate our deliberations."

Says the Head Juror.

Juror 10 remarks:

"Based on the facts. The defendant claimed the pastor and his wife stated they were there first. What if they shot him? They, according to a detailed statement: They arrived while both officers blood was still warm and pumping. She reiterated that's the statement the pastor gave to the police, while detained with his wife shaking like a leaf on a tree, at the Police Station. What about that Glock found at his church?"

Juror 12 is on her feet.

"Mr. Head Juror, you stated a while ago, this thing could go for weeks or even months. Please understand, this trial is not paid for in Jamaican dollars. Jamaicans are proud people.

Judge Lopez should have known this could cost a fortune; even if Jamaicans are more sympathetic with their kind.

This trial should never pan out in the United States of America. In God we trust. US taxpayers shouldn't have to foot this bill. Let Sandals of Jamaica pick up the tab."

Juror # 3 is adamant. He gets up from the table and paces back and forth.

Juror 3 states:

"I like that Marcus Davis' testimony. The man who was incarcerated and lived on the same cell block as Gregg Nichols, the husband of Yuki Nichols.

Marcus Davis testified: One day he and Gregg Nichols were playing dominoes. Nichols boasted about his new hit album. Yet, in the can. As he stated: His wife wouldn't let go of the Sponji Edwards affair. The Glock reconstruction expert.

He also bragged about the relationship between Yuki and Rose Best-Parsons.

Davis said he asked Gregg Nichols how long Rose Best-Parsons was associated with his wife Deja aka Yuki? Gregg Nichols responded: Their relationship began after Wesley and Britney Haynes failed to reproduce a scratched-up CD containing their hit song.

Deja introduced Rose to her producer, a musician who was blind from birth."

Juror 7 shows impartiality.

"According to Marcus Davis, and I'm reading from my notes."

Says Juror 3.

The pad from which he reads is moist from sweaty palms.

He continues.

"Gregg Nichols said: It is no happenstance, Rose Best-Parsons acquired a reconstructed Glock handgun. Deja not only spearheaded the operation and if I had a friend who needed to be armed. I would have readily armed her.

When Marcus Davis was asked if he believed the late Gregg Nichols? He said he didn't have a reason to lie. There was much on Gregg's chest as he tried hard to get acquitted. Even if he had to throw his wife Deja under the bus."

Juror 7 remains independent.

"I don't believe in any of Marcus Davis' testimony. I don't see why you took those notes. Marcus Davis is a traitor, a Con Man, a known liar. In the trial Gregg Nichols vs Who Shot The Sheriff?

And I cite: Marcus Davis testified: Nichols, while in prison, told him how he methodically orchestrated the assassination of Milton Rogers.

He made it a clean sweep. Subsequently, Gregg Nichols was acquitted and Court Officer Quentin Daley was implicated in that assassination."

CHAPTER 28

Juror 2 seems wearied. He gets a drink of water from the fountain.

"There are way too many entanglements in this case.

It becomes visible the Head Juror is pressed and looking everywhere for answers."

Head Juror asks:

"Have we really examined the defendant's state of mind?"

Juror 2 responds:

"I don't know if that will prove anything. Her mind was to be a cop killer."

Head Juror states:

"At the time of her arrest, she claimed: The gun could have belonged to her husband Bill Parsons. He was accustomed to arming himself. Her statement revealed. When asked why it was inside the car which she drove? The defendant said: I was cleaning out my car. Saw the pistol. Moved it over so I could get enough space to fit my large bottle of hand lotion..."

Juror 3 interjects.

"So, she came upon a gun in her car. She didn't put it there as she claimed. Why didn't she call in the police to remove it? If she didn't want to have anything to do with guns?"

Juror 12 states:

"I'm afraid of snakes. If I find a snake inside my car. The first thing I do is scream bloody murder. Secondly, after regaining my presence of mind, I'll call for help to remove it. Touching it is a no, no."

Juror 7 counteracts.

"A gun is not a snake. It's a serpent. A snake moves of its own accord. A gun moves when its aided by movement. The defendant could have ignored it. Sensing, it was a treasured means of protection."

Head Juror asks:

"Did the defendant "know" or "appreciate" that her conduct at the time of storing an illegal weapon was right? Additionally, to desire to use it? Was she "compelled" to use the weapon to commit the criminal act? Did the defendant "premeditate" the crime? She was alleged to have spoken at length with others regarding her distaste for the Sheriff. Was she aware of the risks her conduct posed? Did the defendant Rose Best-Parsons really feel that harm was imminent and that violence was the only way to take action against Sheriff John Brown?"

Juror 8 goes to her notes.

"Her chauffeur, Big Bubba, testified the defendant did on numerous occasions shared her dislike for the Sheriff. Even though he said he didn't see her commit the murders or believed it is something she was capable of pulling off. Even if you gave her a belt, I don't think she could have killed a fly. Much less two. In my view, that best fits this narrative."

Juror 12 is furious.

"You are kidding me! So, are you prepared for allowing this multi-cop killer to go free? So, she can take out any law enforcement individual, she's not too happy with? What are we proposing? If a cop cites a motorist for running the red light. We, instead of going to court and at least fight the ticket. We build up a hated nexus. Stalk him and eventually guns him down? I did not sign up for this. Locked in a stuffy room for hours and hours. I hate being sequestered. Challenged by a judge to come up with a unanimous verdict. When this deliberation all began, we were closer to the truth. Now everything seems to be diluted like ink saturated with water. Look at where we've gotten. Our decision has swayed. Our taxpayers are being mugged. If flipping was an easy thing... I don't mean that, please allow me to walk it back. All those of you who flipped on the government's case. Should be ashamed of yourselves. At this point, my vote is still guilty."

CHAPTER 29

Juror 8 looks at Juror 12 intently.

Why don't you just go over the edge and flip? Don't you see you are the only woman still holding out? This is the age of ME TOO!

Juror 2 states:

"I had no idea the results of this deliberation were based on gender."

Eyes are now focused on Juror 6.

Juror 6 states:

"Why am I being targeted? Because I'm the minority inside the room?"

Juror 8 says to Juror 6.

"You are neither a witness, a subject nor a target."

Then to Juror 2.

"I had no idea it was based on if the Heat beat up on the Knicks during the last two minutes of the game."

Head Juror tries to maintain a calm deliberation.

"Okay. Our duty here is to find a story which assimilates the known facts more completely, more consistently and with fewer inferences. Although there might be competing stories. We need to find one we all can agree on."

Juror 12 picks up from where she was cut off.

"The defendant was found with a Glock in her possession. It wasn't in her hands but in the glove compartment of her automobile. She claimed she didn't know how it got there. It could have been placed there before she became a widow. Two cops were shot months prior to this gun possession incident. She didn't have a prior criminal record. Squeaky clean. Except for a possibly manufactured moving violation."

Juror 2 eyes the clock.

Juror 12 continues.

"Probably she never used a handgun. Maybe someone who interacted with her did shed her hair sample in their vehicle or she rode in that SUV at some point, refreshed her lips and forgot her lip gloss upon exiting. That hypothetical is unique, economic, coherent and consistent with the defendant's character. Therefore, I'll have to change my vote to not guilty."

Juror 2 responds:

"I saw that coming. Now we are getting higher and higher toward hanging ourselves."

Several jurors voting guilty toss their notepads and pens on the table and walk away. The head juror tries to bring calm to the deliberations. The court officer peaks inside wondering what has transpired.

Head Juror prompts.

"Don't worry about it. A slight disagreement just seemed to have gotten some members rattled. I've got this. Thanks for all you do."

Head Juror closes the door. He goes to the board and writes 4-8.

Juror 2, still high-wired.

"Moments ago, those numbers were reversed."

Juror 2 walks away from the table. He goes to the same window. Pops another Nicorette gum.

The Head Juror is entirely focused. He discusses.

Rose Best-Gordon had the right to see what evidence the prosecution had against her before the trial. Which means she had rights to discovery in the case. Have we focused on her alibi? Where was the defendant? If she said she's not guilty. Where was she?

Juror 7 defends.

"She wasn't there. There's no evidence placing her at the scene of the crime. It's all circumstantial. What ifs. Like the pretense in a good crime novel.

Juror 2 asks,
"Really?"

CHAPTER 30

The Head Juror peruses through his multiple notepads.

"Okay. Let's revisit the circumstances. Sheriff John Brown and his Deputy Ron Charles are conducting a traffic watch. The light changes from yellow to red. A black SUV speeds through the intersection. The two Sheriff cars are not waiting for the traffic signal to change. They take off in pursuit of the vehicle…

Sheriff Browns' car ahead of the pack now with flashing lights and sirens are in chase of the eluding motorist. Deputy Ron Charles car follows suits with flashing emergency signals. Finally, the luxury vehicle stops and waits on the right shoulder…"

Juror 8 interrupts.

That motorist wasn't the defendant Rose Best-Parsons. It had to be someone else."

Head Juror counters.

"The two officers dart out of their vehicle with guns pointed towards the idle SUV. As both men got closer to the parked vehicle, two rounds of gunshots in quick succession cut them down to the ground from through the vehicle's rear windscreen. The luxury vehicle takes off in speed leaving Sheriff Brown and his deputy Ron Charles bloodied and lifeless on the street. The vehicle races unaccompanied through the streets of Mandeville…"

Juror 12 interrupts.

"That sounds like something a known, skilled criminal would do. The defendant was unskilled…remember?"

The Head Juror continues with his summation.

"Detective Paul Stevens testified that he and detective Jones were called to the crime scene that night of the murders. He stated that when he arrived, he interviewed an elderly couple, who called 119, stating that on their way home from church they saw what looked like an accident. The couple Claude and Doris Weeks further stated: They got out of their car to see if someone needed an ambulance or CPR. At that point, they saw the two officers lying there dead along the roadside…"

Juror 7 interjects.

"Claude Weeks died after he was charged with the murders. His wife was not called to testify. Why?"

Juror 2 states:

"Let the HJ finish. That's why he was appointed. Keep going…Mr. Chairman.

Head Juror continues.

"The couple said that they figured that the officers had been shot as their bodies seemed pierced, one in the neck and the other in the head. They also claimed that they smelled sulfuric fumes like gun powder. It then was confirmed in their minds the men could have been shot."

Juror 4 removes his glasses, polishes then thoroughly, inspect them. Satisfied, he returns then to his face during the Head Juror's disputation.

"Detective Jones and Stevens wanted to believe the couple but had to perform their duty. So, detective Jones and Stevens, according to their corroborated testimony had the couple transported to the police station. There we later questioned the couple more extensively and released them. The two detectives testified."

Juror 7 gets up and paces the room. He finally takes his seat.

Head Juror notices his move and continues.

"The time of deaths determined by the autopsy, indicated that the deaths could have occurred between 8:30 PM and 8:35 PM. Detective Stevens further testified: They arrived at the crime scene at about 9:15 PM."

The Head Juror takes his seat.

JUROR 7 quickly relinquishes his seat at the table. He Filibusters and then presides.

"Yes. The Coroner testified and let me unpack: Sheriff John Brown died at 8:33 PM. His Deputy died two minutes later at 8:35 PM. Bubba, the chauffeur for the defendant testified: he dropped her off at the Salon at 8:30 PM."

"Where is he taking this?"

Asks Juror 4. He then focuses on Juror 7.

"Are you her lawyer?"

Juror 7 pays no attention to Juror 4's pompousness. Instead, he goes to the board and outlines:

"The distance between the Beauty Salon and the Crime Scene is at least fifteen miles. It seems quite unlikely, she could have committed these murders, dispose of the SUV in a ravine. Have her chauffeur pick her up and drops the defendant her off at the Salon. There goes her alibi. Based on that alone. Rose Best-Gordon is not guilty."

Juror 4 remarks.

"At this point after hearing those facts. I have no choice but to change my vote. She was not capable of undertaking such a task."

Juror 2 yells.

"You did? Holy smokes!"

Juror 4 responds:

"Yep. I'm all in. Count the chips."

Head Juror asks:

"Okay. Is there anyone else siding with the not guilty vote?"

Had Juror is back is on his feet.

Juror 5 raises his hand.

"I'm leaning towards it but I'm still doubtful based on her motives. She categorically despised the Sheriff. On the other hand, Sponji Edwards started this whole thing. It could have been him. He was able to make his guns and bullets untraceable. His proficiency scares me. How did he do it?"

Juror 7 states:

Easy. Firstly, he discovered. Secondly, he tested and thirdly, he pattern - set.

Juror 7 returns to his seat.

Head Juror asks.

"Juror 5 you look puzzled."

Juror 5 answers.

"I am."

Head Juror asks.

"Okay. So, where do you really stand?"

Juror 5 focuses on the other jurors all seated except for the Head Juror.

Juror 5 states.

"I have to say, I've changed my mind. I have to change my vote. I need to stop fighting my conscience. I vote not guilty."

Juror 2 is inflexible.

"Why didn't you say that all along? You raved, you spun, and now you caved. Very wishy-washy. Now it's 3-9 in favor of the NGs."

Juror 5 responds.

"At least I'm man enough to be able to walk something back."

Juror 2 asks:

"Yeah? What if the defendant was to walk in this room right now and said she would like to walk back her statements?"

The Head Juror assures:

"That would make all of our jobs easier. Don't you think?"

Juror 2 responds:

"I'm thinking. Hypothetically, if we all consented to send that poor woman to the electric chair and later found out it wasn't, she who did those killings? That would brand us the worse 12 jurors on the planet. I can't go down that road. I change my vote.

Head Juror states:

"Even if everyone else disagrees. I am holding out..."

Suddenly, the main door opens of its own accord.

The JURORS are rattled.

Except for the HEAD JUROR. He states and writes on the board in all caps and quotations:

"DEAD MEN TELL NO TALES!"

ABOUT THE AUTHOR

John A. Andrews hails from the beautiful Islands of St. Vincent and the Grenadines and resides in Hollywood, California. He is best known for his gritty and twisted writing style in his National Bestselling novel - Rude Buay ... The Unstoppable. He is in (2012) releasing this chronicle in the French edition, and poised to release its sequel Rude Buay ... The Untouchable in March 2012.

Andrews moved from New York to Hollywood in 1996, to pursue his acting career. With early success, he excelled as a commercial actor. Then tragedy struck - a divorce, with Andrews, granted joint custody of his three sons, Jonathan, Jefferri, and Jamison, all under the age of five. That dream of becoming all he could be in the entertainment industry now took on nightmarish qualities.

In 2002, after avoiding bankruptcy and a twisted relationship at his modeling agency, he fell in love with a 1970s classic film, which he wanted to remake. Subsequent to locating the studio which held those rights, his request was denied. As a result, Andrews decided that he was going to write his own. Not knowing how to write and failing constantly at it, he inevitably recorded his first bestseller, Rude Buay ... The Unstoppable in 2010: a drug prevention chronicle, sending a strong message to teens and adults alike

Andrews is also a visionary, and a prolific author who has etched over two dozen titles including: Dare to Make a Difference - Success 101 for Teens, The 5 Steps To Changing Your Life, Spread Some Love - Relationships 101, Quotes Unlimited, How I Wrote 8 Books in One Year, The FIVE "Ps" for Teens, Total Commitment - The Mindset of Champions, and Whose Woman Was She? - A True Hollywood Story.

In 2007, Mr. Andrews a struggling actor and author etched his first book The 5 Steps to Changing Your Life. That title having much to do with changing one's thoughts, words, actions, character and changing the world. A book which he claims shaped his life as an author with now over two dozen published titles.

Andrews followed up his debut title with Spread Some Love - Relationships 101 in 2008, a title which he later turned into a one-hour docu-drama.

Additionally, during that year, Andrews wrote eight titles, including Total Commitment - The Mindset of Champions, Dare to Make A Difference - Success 101 for Teens, Spread Some Love - Relationships 101 (Workbook) and Quotes Unlimited.

After those publications in 2009, Andrews recorded his hit novel as well as Whose Woman Was She? and When the Dust Settles - I am Still Standing: his True Hollywood Story, now also being turned into a film.

New titles in the Personal Development genre include Quotes Unlimited Vol. II, The FIVE "Ps" For Teens, Dare to Make A Difference - Success 101 and Dare to Make A Difference - Success 101 - The Teacher's Guide.

His new translated titles include Chico Rudo ... El Imparable, Cuya Mujer Fue Ella? and Rude Buay ... The Unstoppable in Chinese.

Back in 2009, while writing the introduction of his debut book for teens: Dare To Make A Difference - Success 101 for Teens, Andrews visited the local bookstore. He discovered only 5 books in the Personal Development genre for teens while noticing hundreds of the same genre in the adult section. Sensing there was a lack of personal growth resources, focusing on youth 13-21, he published his teen book and soon thereafter founded Teen Success.

This organization is empowerment based, designed to empower Teens in maximizing their full potential to be successful and contributing citizens in the world.
Andrews referred to as the man with "the golden voice" is a sought after speaker on "Success" targeting young adults. He recently addressed teens in New York, Los Angeles, Hawaii and was the guest speaker at the 2011 Dr. Martin Luther King Jr. birthday celebrations in Eugene, Oregon.

John Andrews came from a home of educators; all five of his sisters taught school - two acquiring the status of school principals. Though self-educated, he understands the benefits of a great education and being all he can be. Two of his teenage sons are also writers. John spends most of his time writing, publishing books and traveling the country going on book tours.

Additionally, John Andrews is a screenwriter and producer and is in (2012) turning his bestselling novel into a film.

See more in: HOW I RAISED MYSELF FROM FAILURE TO SUCCESS IN HOLLYWOOD.

Visit: www.JohnAAndrews.com

Check out Upcoming Titles & New Releases...

<u>UPCOMING RELEASE</u>

DESIREE O'GARRO

THE LETHAL KID

A TEEN THRILLER

FROM THE CREATORS OF

RUDE BUAY
AGENT O'GARRO
RENEGADE COPS
A SNITCH ON TIME
WHO SHOT THE SHERIFF?
&
*THE MACOS ADVENTURE

#1 INTERNATIONAL BESTSELLING AUTHOR

JOHN A. ANDREWS

&

·JEFFERRI ANDREWS

A TEEN-FRIENDLY NOVEL

WHEN SEASONS CHANGE

#1 INTERNATIONAL BESTSELLING AUTHOR

JOHN A. ANDREWS

&

DELROY LINGO

NEW RELEASES

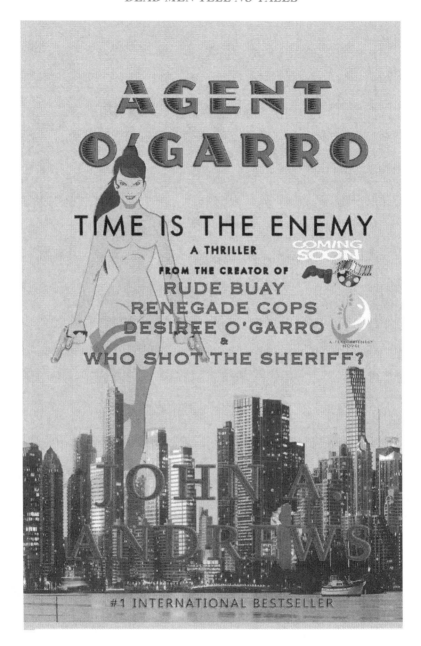

OTHER RELEASES

AUTHOR OF THE RUDE BUAY SERIES

JOHN A. ANDREWS
A MEMOIR IN TWO VOLUMES

HOW I RAISED MYSELF

FROM FAILURE TO SUCCESS

IN HOLLYWOOD

How I Wrote 8 Books In One Year

JOHN A.
ANDREWS

A

Author of
TOTAL COMMITTMENT
The Mindset Of Champions

ANDREWS

"QUOTES"

UNLIMITED

Vol. II

Over 400 Quotes From Over 18 Books!

John A. Andrews

National Bestselling Author of

RUDE BUAY ... THE UNSTOPPABLE

National Bestselling Author of
Rude Buay ... The Unstoppable

THE 5
STEPS TO
CHANGING
YOUR LIFE
BY: JOHN A. ANDREWS

JOHN A. ANDREWS

THE MUSICAL©

FROM THE CREATOR OF
RUDE BUAY
THE WHODUNIT CHRONICLES
&
THE CHURCH ON FIRE

SO MANY ARE TRYING TO GO TO HEAVEN
WITHOUT FIRST BUILDING A HEAVEN
HERE ON EARTH...
#1 INTERNATIONAL BESTSELLER

JOHN A. ANDREWS

CREATOR OF:
THE CHURCH ... A HOSPITAAL?
&
THE CHURCH ON FIRE

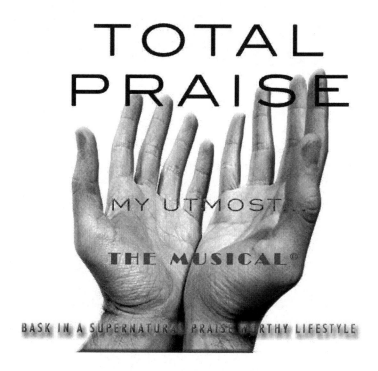

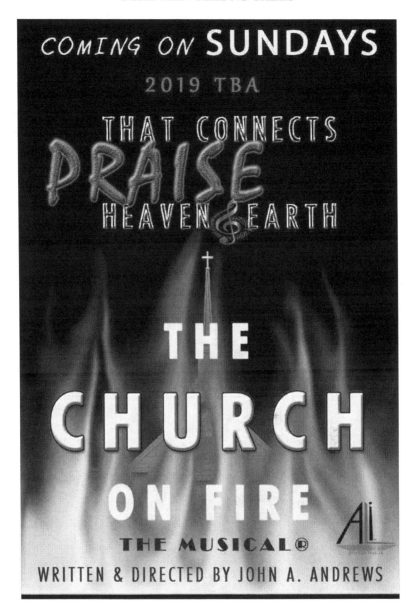

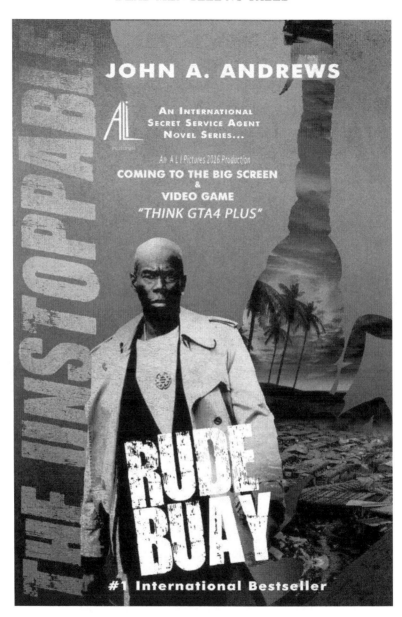

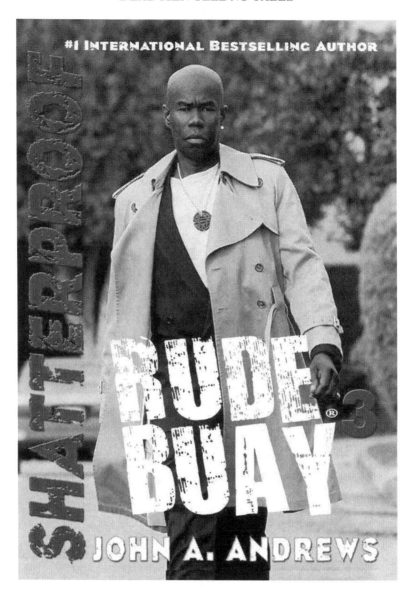

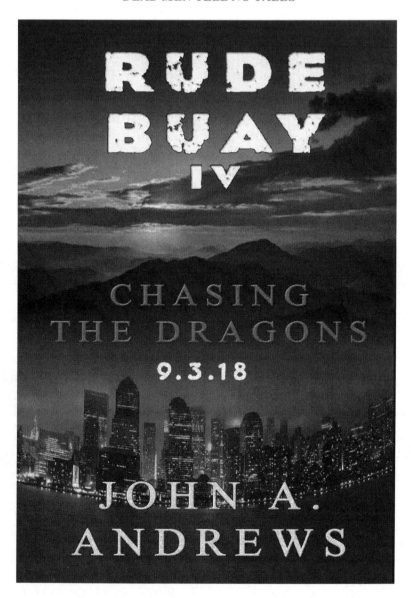

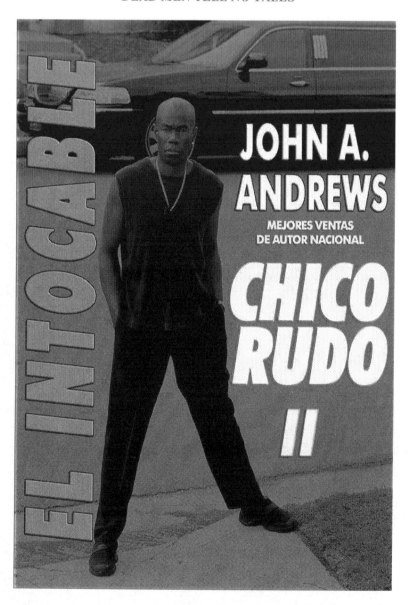

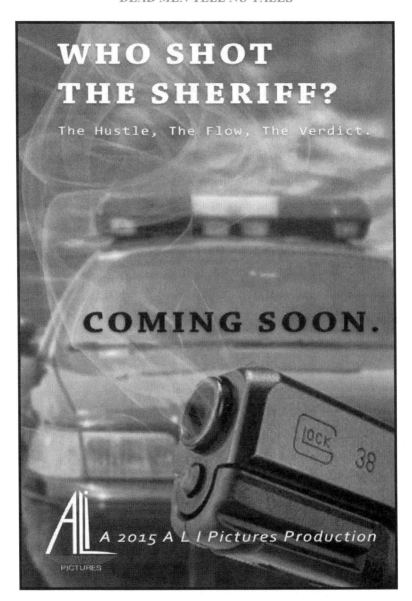

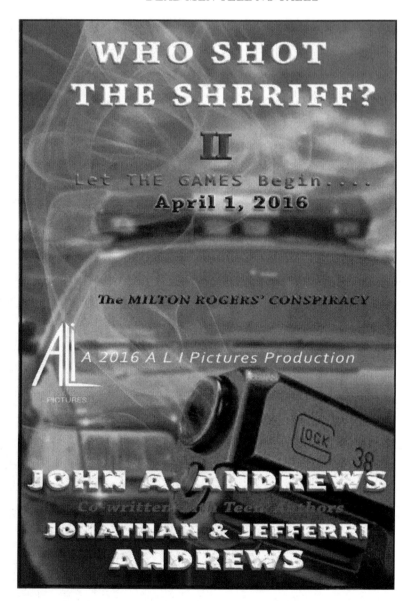

VISIT: WWW.JOHNAANDREWS.COM

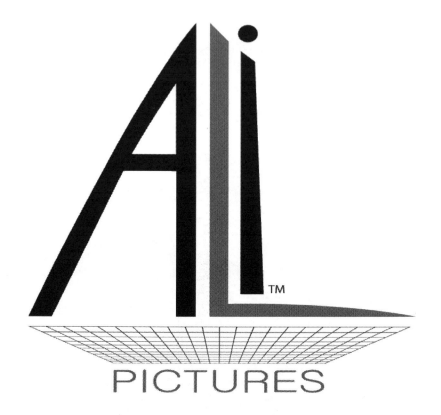

Optioned by A L I Pictures, LLC.

LIKE Us on FaceBook

https://www.facebook.com/Whoshotthesherifffilm

53119469R00100

Made in the USA
Lexington, KY
29 September 2019